Here's what kids have to say to
Mary Pope Osborne, author of
the Magic Tree House series:

I want you to write 999,999,999,999,999 books.
—Tyler C.

I let my teacher read one of your books. She said it was her most favorite book.— Jackie P.

I love your books so much! My favorite is all of them!—Lauren D.

I love your Magic Tree House series. I feel as if I could walk right through the books.—Levi H.

I wish I could collect every one of your books, and I hope you make millions more.—Claire M.

Whenever I read a Magic Tree House book, it makes my mind go off on an adventure.— Jeff D.

I wish I could spend my life reading the Magic Tree House series.— Juliette S.

I really like your Magic Tree House books. They are making me happier than a hyena.
—Natalie D.

Parents and teachers love Magic Tree House books, too!

As a parent, I thank you for writing stories filled with adventures, fun, and valuable lessons.—M. Nagao

You have made a reader out of my 8-year-old son! I had the thrilling experience yesterday of watching him walk from the car to the front door, his nose in your book the whole way.—M. Houghton

Your Magic Tree House series may inspire me to go back and teach elementary students and gear an entire curriculum around your series!—J. Hendrickson

Thanks for writing such great books! Not only have your books motivated our class to want to read better, but our class has motivated other classes to do the same! At least six other classrooms have ordered the Magic Tree House books for next year.
—Mrs. Kennedy

My class has just discovered your wonderful Magic Tree House series! They are thrilled, scared, entertained, and mesmerized by the adventures of Jack and Annie!
—B. Paget-Puppa

I can't tell you how much my students' success at reading the Magic Tree House books has had an impact upon their learning in other classrooms. I even have parents calling me to inquire what I have done to their child, who previously didn't know how to read!—P. Lorensen

Dear Readers,

During the past year, many of my readers have requested that Jack and Annie visit the _Titanic_. At first, I thought the story was too sad. However, as more and more requests came in, I began to think about it, for I take the suggestions of kids very seriously. So I tried to think of a way that Jack and Annie might actually be helpful in the midst of such a tragedy. I talked about my ideas with a lot of kids, including my nephews, Peter and Andrew. Finally, I decided to go ahead and write the story.

Now I'm glad I did. While researching the true story of the _Titanic_, I learned a lot about human dignity and courage in the face of disaster. So I thank all the readers who wrote a letter or raised a hand in a school assembly or sent an e-mail to our Web site that said, "Please write a Magic Tree House book about the _Titanic_." This one's for you.

All my best,

Mary Pope Osborne

Tonight on the Titanic

by Mary Pope Osborne

illustrated by
Sal Murdocca

A STEPPING STONE BOOK™

Random House 🏠 New York

For Bailey,
the magic terrier in my life

Text copyright © 1999 by Mary Pope Osborne.
Illustrations copyright © 1999 by Sal Murdocca.

www.randomhouse.com/kids

Library of Congress Cataloging-in-Publication Data

Osborne, Mary Pope.
Tonight on the Titanic / by Mary Pope Osborne ; illustrated by Sal Murdocca.
p. cm. — (Magic tree house ; #17) "A stepping stone book." Summary: The magic
tree house transports Jack and Annie to the deck of the *Titanic* to find a mysterious
gift that will free their puppy from a terrible magic spell.
ISBN 0-679-89063-7 (pbk.) — ISBN 0-679-99063-1 (lib. bdg.)
1. Titanic (Steamship)—Juvenile fiction. [1. Titanic (Steamship)—Fiction.
2. Shipwrecks—Fiction. 3. Survival—Fiction. 4. Time travel—Fiction.
5. Magic—Fiction.]
I. Murdocca, Sal, ill. II. Title. III. Series: Osborne, Mary Pope. Magic tree house
series ; #17. PZ7.081167To 1999 [Fic]—dc21 98-31007

Printed in the United States of America 19 18 17 16 15 14 13 12 11 10

Random House, Inc. New York, Toronto, London, Sydney, Auckland

Contents

Tonight on the Titanic

Prologue

One day in Frog Creek, Pennsylvania, a mysterious tree house appeared in the woods.

Eight-year-old Jack and his seven-year-old sister, Annie, climbed into the tree house. They found that it was filled with books.

Jack and Annie soon discovered that

the tree house was magic. It could take them to the places in the books. All they had to do was point to a picture and wish to go there.

Along the way, they discovered that the tree house belongs to Morgan le Fay. Morgan is a magical librarian from the time of King Arthur. She travels through time and space, gathering books.

In Magic Tree House Books #5–8, Jack and Annie helped free Morgan from a spell. In books #9–12, they solved four ancient riddles and became Master Librarians.

In Magic Tree House Books #13–16, Jack and Annie had to save four ancient stories from being lost forever.

Now, in book #17, they are about to begin
a new set of adventures...

1

A New Mission

Jack opened his eyes.

It was a stormy night. The rain tapped hard on his window pane.

"Do you hear what the rain is saying?" said a voice.

Jack turned on his lamp.

Annie stood in his doorway. She wore her rain poncho over her pajamas and held a flashlight.

"It's saying, *Come now!*" she said.

"You're nuts," said Jack.

"Listen, just listen," said Annie.

Jack listened.

The rain *did* seem to be tapping out *Come now! Come now!*

"We *have* to go to the tree house," said Annie. "Something important is about to happen."

"Now?" said Jack.

Jack didn't want to leave his warm, cozy room. But he had a feeling Annie was right. Something important *was* about to happen.

"You coming?" she said.

"Yeah, yeah," he said.

He climbed out of bed.

"Just put on your rain poncho," said Annie.

Jack threw his rain poncho over his

pajamas. He pulled on his sneakers and grabbed his backpack.

"Don't forget your Master Librarian card," said Annie. "I have mine with me."

Jack put the card with the glowing letters **ML** on it into his backpack.

"I'm ready," he said.

Jack and Annie went quietly down the stairs. Then they slipped out the door into the chilly, damp night.

The storm had eased up. Rain fell gently as they ran up the street. The wet ground glistened in the beam of the flashlight.

They headed into the Frog Creek woods. Wind blew through the trees, shaking water to the ground.

Jack shivered. He wiped raindrops off his glasses.

"Brrr," said Annie. "I'm cold."

"Me too," said Jack.

As they kept walking, Annie pointed the flashlight up into the trees.

"There it is," she said. Her light had found the tree house.

"Morgan!" Jack called.

There was no answer.

"I wonder what's wrong," said Annie. "I was sure she'd be here."

"Let's go up and see," said Jack.

Annie grabbed the rope ladder and started climbing.

Jack followed. Rain dripped from the trees onto his poncho.

They climbed into the tree house. Annie shined her light into each corner. The first three corners were empty.

Then the flashlight beam hit the fourth. Jack and Annie gasped with surprise.

Sitting in the corner was a small dog. He looked like a terrier puppy. He had scruffy light brown fur.

He stared sadly at Jack and Annie.

"Oh!" whispered Annie.

"Where did you come from?" said Jack.

Annie patted the dog's head. He wagged his tail.

"He's so cute," she said. "He looks like a little teddy bear. Hi, Teddy."

Teddy was actually a good name for him, Jack thought.

"Where did you come from, Teddy?" he asked.

The little dog whimpered.

"Don't be sad," said Annie. "Everything's okay."

"How did he get up here?" Jack asked.

"I don't know. But I bet Morgan had some-thing to do with it," said Annie.

Jack's gaze fell on a piece of paper lying on the floor.

"I think you're right," he said.

He picked up the paper. On it was fancy
writing that said:

*This little dog is under a spell and needs
your help. To free him, you must be given
four special things:*

A gift from a ship lost at sea,
A gift from the prairie blue,
A gift from a forest far away,
A gift from a kangaroo.
Be wise. Be brave. Be careful.
                    Morgan

*P.S. Your Master Librarian cards won't help
on this mission. Just be yourselves and all
will be well.*

"What kind of spell do you think Teddy is
under?" said Annie.

"Who knows?" said Jack.

"Poor thing," said Annie. She patted the dog's head. He licked her hand.

"It looks like we have to take four trips," said Jack.

Teddy trotted over to a book. He pushed it with his nose.

"Look!" said Annie. "I bet *that* will take us on the first trip."

She picked up the book that the little dog had chosen.

"Good job, Teddy," she said.

The title of the book was *The Unsinkable Ship*.

"Well, at least that's good," said Jack. "The ship won't sink, even if it *is* lost."

"Ready, Teddy?" asked Annie.

"*Arf! Arf!*" he answered.

Jack pointed at the cover of the book.

"I wish we could go there," he said.

The wind started to blow.

The tree house started to spin.

It spun faster and faster.

Then everything was still.

Absolutely still.

2

The Unsinkable Ship

"Arf! Arf!?"

Jack opened his eyes. He shivered. Wherever they were now, it was cold—*very* cold.

Teddy barked again.

"Shhh," said Jack.

Annie shined the flashlight on her clothes.

"Wow, we're dressed like old-fashioned kids!" she said.

Instead of pajamas and a poncho, she wore a sailor dress and a long wool cloak.

14

Jack had on an overcoat and knee-length pants with long socks. His backpack had turned to leather. He also had on a shirt and tie.

"Where are we?" he wondered aloud.

Jack and Annie looked out the window.

The moonless sky glittered with stars.

There was a soft wind and the sound of water lapping.

The tree house seemed to be resting on a wooden deck between two giant columns.

Jack looked up and saw smoke coming out of the columns.

"We must have landed on the ship between the smokestacks," he said.

Then Jack looked straight ahead and saw a box high in the air, near the front of the ship.

"That must be the lookouts' nest," he said.

Jack sat back in the tree house and opened their book. Annie handed him the flashlight.

"Let's find out where we are," he said.

He turned to a picture of a huge ocean liner. By the light of the flashlight, he read:

> Late at night, on April 14, 1912, an English ocean liner was making her first voyage across the Atlantic Ocean. She was going to New York City. Carrying 2,200 passengers, the ship was four city blocks long. Most people believed the ship was unsinkable.

"Oh, man, we're in 1912," said Jack. He pulled out his notebook and wrote:

April 14, 1912

"This ship is huge," said Annie. "How will we ever find the gift to help free Teddy?"

"You can't go looking for a gift," said Jack. "You have to wait until someone gives it to you."

"Right," said Annie with a sigh. "Well, I guess we just have to be ourselves, like Morgan said. And maybe we'll get lucky."

"This is hard," said Jack.

The little dog whined.

"Don't worry, Teddy," said Annie. "We'll free you from your spell."

Just then, a shout came from the lookouts' nest: "Iceberg ahead!"

Jack and Annie turned back to the window—just in time to see a huge iceberg looming out of the sea.

The iceberg was dark with a fringe of white at the top. And it was right in front of the ship!

Jack felt a jolt. Then he heard a grinding sound. The ship was scraping against the mountain of ice.

"*Arf! Arf!*" Teddy barked.

"Shhh, don't be scared," said Annie.

She picked the dog up and hugged him.

The scraping sound stopped. The ship slid past the iceberg until they lost sight of it.

The night was calm again.

"See?" Annie said to Teddy. "It was just a little bump. This ship is unsinkable."

But Jack was worried. "Wait. I have to read more about this," he said.

"Don't read now, Jack," said Annie. "It's time to get the gift. Come on, Teddy."

She picked up the little dog and the flashlight. And she climbed out the tree house window.

"Hey—don't take the flashlight!" said Jack.

But Annie was gone.

"Annie!" called Jack.

He heard a soft "Yikes."

Annie stuck her head back in the tree house.

"Bad news," she said in a whisper. "I think you'd better see this."

Jack threw his stuff into his knapsack. He put it on and climbed out the window.

Annie was standing by the ship's railing, holding Teddy.

Without a word, she shined the flashlight on a life preserver hanging from the railing.

In big black letters were the words:

R.M.S. TITANIC

3

SOS

Jack stared at the name of the ship.

"You know what happened to the *Titanic*, don't you?" he said softly.

Annie nodded.

"It hit an iceberg and sank," she said. "But I don't get it. I thought this ship was unsinkable."

"That's what people thought when the *Titanic* was built," said Jack. "But they were wrong."

Suddenly, steam gushed out of the ship's smokestacks. Then the engines cut off. The *Titanic* stopped moving.

"We'd better go home," said Jack. "There's nothing we can do here. We'll have to find another lost ship—a safer one."

"No! We have to stay and help," said Annie. "We can escape in the tree house anytime we want."

"But what can we do?" said Jack. "This ship's going to sink no matter what. We can't change history. And we can't take anyone into our time with us."

"Yeah, but maybe there's some way we can help," said Annie.

"How?" said Jack.

"I don't know," said Annie. "Let's look around." Holding Teddy, she disappeared down a small stairway.

Jack followed her to a lower level.

Annie put Teddy down on the deck. The dog sniffed the chunks of ice that had fallen off the iceberg.

The ship seemed strangely empty.

"Where is everyone?" Annie asked.

"Maybe they're still asleep," said Jack. "They probably don't even know the ship hit something."

Annie and Jack started toward the front of the *Titanic*.

"Come on, Teddy," said Annie.

The little dog scampered after them.

They passed the round windows of different rooms on the ship. Jack looked through them as they went by.

He saw exercise bikes and rowing

machines in one room. In another, there were palm trees, bamboo chairs, and tables. Next, they passed a library filled with books.

"This ship is like a town," said Jack.

Near the end of the deck, they peeked through another round window. Inside a little room, a man was wearing earphones.

Jack heard a clicking noise as the man tapped a lever on a black box.

"What's he doing?" whispered Annie.

Jack shrugged.

Another man stood nearby. He had a white beard and wore a fancy uniform.

"Send the international call for help," he ordered the man with headphones. "Tell all ships close by to come at once. We're sinking."

"Yes, Captain," said the man.

"Great, they're calling for help!" Annie whispered.

Jack shook his head. "I don't think help will come," he said.

He shined the flashlight on the book and found a picture of the radio operator.

He read quietly to Annie:

> After the *Titanic* hit the iceberg at 11:40 P.M., the ship's radio operator sent out an SOS. An SOS is the international distress signal in Morse code. Unfortunately, the only ship near the *Titanic* had turned off its radio for the night. All the other ships who received the message were too far away to help. When the *Titanic* sank around 2:20 A.M., she was all alone.

"That's terrible," said Annie.

"I wonder what time it is now," said Jack.

"I don't know," said Annie.

Jack pulled out his notebook and wrote:

SOS sent out
Titanic sinks at 2:20 A.M.

"He's leaving," whispered Annie.

"Hide!" whispered Jack.

He and Annie moved quickly into the shadows.

The captain stepped out onto the deck.

"Tell the men to start loading the lifeboats now," the captain ordered a deck hand.

"Yes, Captain!" the man answered.

The captain and the deck hand left. Annie turned to Jack.

"At least that's good," she whispered. "Everyone can get into the lifeboats."

"I don't think it's good enough," said Jack. He read from the book again:

On the *Titanic*, there were 20
lifeboats. To save all the passengers,
the ship needed twice as many. But
with all the confusion on board, a
number of the lifeboats were not even
full when they left the ship. Many
third-class passengers did not have a
chance to get into any of the lifeboats
because they were on the lower decks
and didn't know where to go.

Jack wrote in his notebook:

Need twice as many lifeboats

"Hey, I know what we can do to help," said
Annie.

"What?" asked Jack.

"We can help someone find the lifeboats,"
she said.

"You're right!" said Jack. "With our book, we can find our way to a lower deck."

He turned the page to a map of the ship. He and Annie studied it.

"We'll start at the grand stairway," said Jack. He traced a path with his finger. "Then we'll go down to the third-class cabins this way."

"Good plan!" said Annie.

Jack looked back through the door. The radio operator was still tapping out his message—over and over and over.

"SOS," whispered Jack.

He took a deep breath.

"Okay," he said. "Let's go."

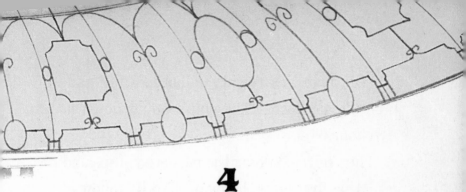

4

Put on Your Life Belts!

Jack and Annie slipped through a door off the boat deck. Teddy was at their heels.

"Wow," breathed Annie.

"*Arf! Arf!*" Teddy barked.

They were at the top of the empty grand stairway. It was beautiful. It was made of dark, glossy wood. A huge dome with lights hung above it.

At the top of the stairs was a fancy clock.

The hands of the clock were at 12:20.

"Oh, man, it's twenty minutes after midnight!" said Jack. "The ship's going down in two hours!"

They hurried down the carpeted steps and into the first-class hallway. Teddy followed along.

Jack looked at the map in the book.

"These are the staterooms," he said. "This hall will take us to the third-class open deck."

"Hey, look," said Annie. "The floor's slanting down."

Jack caught his breath. She was right.

"That means the front of the ship is already sinking," he said.

Just then, a man in a white uniform came down the hall.

He knocked on the doors.

"Put on your life belts at once and come

up to the boat deck!" he called.

Men and women stumbled out of their rooms. They wore elegant robes made of shiny cloth and velvet.

"What's going on?" a woman asked.

"There's been a little accident," the man in the uniform said cheerfully.

"Oh, how silly," said the woman.

"It's not silly!" said Annie. "Do what he says!"

"*Arf! Arf!*" Teddy barked, as if he agreed with Annie.

"Shhh, Teddy!" said Jack.

He picked up the little dog. Then he and Annie hurried down the hall. They crossed the third-class open deck, where more people were standing.

These people were not dressed in fancy

clothes. They mostly wore plain, dark coats. They didn't seem worried either. They were all joking and laughing.

Jack and Annie slipped through the crowd. They went into a big smoky room.

Four men were playing cards.

A woman played the piano. A young couple danced to the music.

"Put on your life belts and go up to the boat deck!" Annie shouted.

The people looked at Annie in surprise. The card players smiled at her.

She opened her mouth to yell again, but Jack pulled her out the door.

"Come on," he said. "We have to get down to the third-class cabins before it's too late."

They hurried down another hall. Then they climbed down another stairway. Jack carried Teddy the whole way.

At the bottom of the stairs, they rounded a corner, and they both gasped.

The floor was *really* slanting down here, and water sloshed at the end of a hallway.

"The *Titanic* is sinking," said Jack.

"But no one understands!" said Annie.

"I know," said Jack. It made him feel terribly sad.

Teddy whined. Jack buried his face in the little dog's fur.

"Come on!" said Annie.

She began banging on the cabin doors.

The doors swung open. The cabins were all empty.

"The people from this hallway must be the ones up near the lounge," said Jack. "Maybe we should go down to a lower deck."

He started to walk back to the stairs. But Teddy began barking furiously.

"What's wrong with him?" said Jack.

"I don't know," said Annie.

Suddenly, the dog leaped out of Jack's arms. He charged down the hall.

He was running straight toward the water!

"Watch out!" cried Jack.

He and Annie ran after Teddy.

The dog began barking at a closed door.

The door opened.

A very small boy peeked out.

5

William and Lucy

The boy wore a nightshirt. He had red hair and freckles. He looked about four years old.

He rubbed his eyes sleepily. Then he saw Teddy.

"Puppy!" he said with a huge smile.

He threw his arms around the little dog's neck. Teddy licked his face.

"Come back to bed, William," a voice called from inside the room.

"Come out!" Annie shouted. "It's an emergency!"

A moment later, the door opened wider. A girl in a long white nightgown peeked out.

She had red hair and freckles, too. She was tall and thin. She looked to be about twelve or thirteen years old.

"Hello," she said. She put her arm around the little boy. "I'm Lucy O'Malley. This is my brother, William."

"I'm Annie," said Annie. "And this is *my* brother, Jack."

"Get your parents and tell them to come with us," said Jack.

Lucy looked confused.

"Our parents aren't here. They're in New York," she said. "We're on our way to them."

"Listen, the *Titanic* has hit an iceberg," said Annie. "We'll take you to a lifeboat."

"What do you mean?" said Lucy.

"The ship's sinking," said Annie. "Look."

She pointed to the water at the end of the hall.

"Oh, no!" cried Lucy.

"Don't be afraid," said Jack. "Just get your coats and your life belts. We don't have much time."

Lucy nodded. Then she went back inside the room and came out with their things.

Lucy pulled on her coat and her life belt. Annie helped William put his on.

"Let's go," said Jack.

"Wait—can Teddy fit in your knapsack?" said Annie.

"Try," said Jack.

Annie slipped the little dog into the leather knapsack on Jack's back. Only Teddy's front paws and head stuck out.

"Stay there, honey," said Annie. She kissed Teddy on the nose.

Jack didn't feel any extra weight in his knapsack. The little dog felt as light as air.

"Wait—I forgot something," said Lucy.

"We don't have time—" started Jack.

But Lucy rushed back into the room.

"Hurry!" shouted Annie.

When Lucy came out, Jack saw her slip something into her coat pocket. Then she grabbed William's hand.

"Ready?" said Jack.

Suddenly, he felt freezing water brush against his shoes.

He looked down. The green sea water was slowly moving down the hall.

"Arf! Arf!" barked Teddy from Jack's pack.

"Run!" cried Annie.

6

Women and Children First

Annie led everyone down the hall to the stairs, away from the cold sea water.

As she and Lucy helped William up the stairs, Jack and Teddy followed.

Halfway up the staircase, Teddy let out a yelp.

Jack looked back.

The water was creeping up the stairs, step by step.

"Come on, Jack!" Annie shouted.

Jack ran up the rest of the stairs.

He and Annie led William and Lucy through the smoky room. The men were still playing cards.

"To the lifeboats!" Annie yelled at the card players. "Right now! Hurry!"

The men smiled at her again.

"Little girl," one said with a laugh, "even if this ship does sink, it will take all night. There's plenty of time for everyone on board to be rescued."

"Indeed. Many ships are on their way right now," another man said in a soothing voice. "There's nothing to worry about."

"Not true!" said Annie.

Lucy turned to Jack.

"This doesn't sound so bad, after all," she said.

"It *is* bad. Please trust me," said Jack. "We have to keep going."

They went outside. The crowd on the third-class deck had grown.

Many wore life belts. But no one here seemed very worried yet.

Jack and Annie pulled Lucy and William along. They hurried through the crowd and down the first-class hall. They came to the end and trooped up the grand staircase.

On the top deck, the *Titanic* was as bright as a Christmas tree.

A band played lively music.

With a hiss and rush of light, a rocket streaked into the sky. It made a loud *boom!* Then it burst into many colored balls.

Shivering in the cold, William laughed and clapped.

"Fireworks!" he said.

Lucy smiled at Jack and Annie.

"This is a trick, isn't it?" she said. "You've brought us to a party."

"No, it isn't," said Jack. "Don't you remember the water downstairs?"

Lucy's smile faded.

"Women and children first!" someone shouted.

"That's you!" said Annie. "Come on!"

She pulled Lucy and William toward a lifeboat.

7

The Gift

The lifeboat was waiting to go down. It looked tiny as it swung on cables at the side of the big ship. The water below looked black.

"Get in! Get in!" a uniformed man shouted.

"No, no," said William. He hid his face against Lucy's coat.

Lucy was shaking her head.

"I'd rather stay here," she said to Jack and Annie.

Jack understood. The brightly lit *Titanic*

seemed so solid and safe compared to the little lifeboat.

"You *can't* stay here," said Annie. "The *Titanic* is going to sink soon."

"*Very* soon," said Jack.

Lucy kept shaking her head. Jack saw tears in her eyes.

"Lucy, we're telling the truth," said Jack. "You and William are in great danger."

"You have to be brave now," said Annie. "For your brother's sake."

Lucy straightened up and tried to smile.

"All right," she said. "I will."

"This way!" a man called. "Women and children! This way, you four!"

He pointed at them.

"Get in," said Jack. He gently pushed Lucy and William forward.

"Good-bye, Lucy," said Annie. "Good-bye, William."

Lucy looked surprised.

"You're not coming?" she asked.

"No, we're going home another way," said Annie.

"Oh, dear," said Lucy. "I hope you'll be safe."

"We will. Don't worry!" said Jack.

"Wait," said Lucy.

She reached into her coat pocket and pulled out a silver watch on a chain.

"This is a gift for both of you," she said. "It's our father's watch. We carried it on the voyage for good luck. I have a feeling that the two of you were our good luck tonight."

Jack looked at the watch as Lucy put it around Annie's neck.

The time on the watch was 1:50.

There were only thirty minutes left!

"Hurry, *hurry!*" he said.

Jack and Annie watched as a big man picked Lucy up and swung her into the little boat. Then he picked William up and put him in Lucy's lap.

"Bye!" cried Annie. She stepped forward to blow a kiss.

Just then, the man picked Annie up.

"No!" shouted Annie.

"Into the lifeboat, my dear!" the man said. And he tossed Annie into the lifeboat.

"No! No!" cried Jack.

Then the man reached for him, too. Jack jumped away just in time.

"Annie!" he yelled. "Get out!"

Annie tried to climb out of the lifeboat.

"Let me out!" she cried.

"*Arf! Arf!*" Teddy barked from over Jack's shoulder.

The lifeboat jerked. It started creaking down toward the dark, cold sea.

"Come back!" Jack called.

But there was nothing he could do as Annie disappeared from sight.

8

Every Man for Himself

"Annie!" cried Jack.

"Let me out!" he heard Annie shout.

But the lifeboat kept going down.

"Wait for me!" came a loud voice. "Wait for me!"

A woman in a fur coat appeared at the railing. She nearly threw herself over the side of the ship.

"Stop!" the uniformed man called. "Bring the boat back up for Lady Blackwell!"

Slowly, the lifeboat was brought back up.

Jack pushed his way forward. The lifeboat came even with the ship. Jack reached out to Annie.

She grabbed his hands. He pulled her back onto the sinking ship.

"Room for one more!" Annie shouted to Lady Blackwell.

Then she and Jack took off before anyone could catch them.

They ran up the slanting deck. Annie stopped and peered over the railing.

Jack looked, too.

They saw Lucy and William's little lifeboat creaking down toward the Atlantic Ocean. It reached the glassy black water. Then it floated off into the darkness.

Annie waved.

"Bye, William! Bye, Lucy!" she shouted. "Thank you for your gift!"

She held up the watch that hung from her neck. Then she and Jack looked at it.

The time was 2:05.

"Only fifteen minutes left!" said Annie.

"We have to get back to the tree house *now*!" said Jack. "Let's climb the stairs to the smokestacks!"

Suddenly, the front of the ship dipped down into the sea. Deck chairs started to slide past Jack and Annie.

The band played a slow, calm song. It sounded like a church hymn.

But the crowd started to panic. People pushed and shouted, trying to get to a safer part of the ship.

"It's every man for himself!" the captain

shouted to all of his crew.

The men all stopped what they were doing
and ran up the deck.

Jack and Annie ran, too.

They dodged sliding tables and chairs.

They reached the stairs that led to the smokestacks.

They grabbed the railing and pulled themselves up the steps.

The ship tilted further.

"Get to those smokestacks!" cried Jack.

They slipped and crawled down the deck.

But when they got to the smokestacks, Jack and Annie looked around wildly.

The magic tree house was gone!

9

Time Stops

"Where is it?" shouted Annie.

The front of the *Titanic* sank deeper into the sea. Jack and Annie fell forward.

They grabbed the railing and held on for their lives.

"Maybe the tree house fell into the ocean!" shouted Jack.

A great roar started coming from the ship.

Jack imagined everything crashing forward—all the furniture, dishes, bicycles, the grand clock on the staircase.

He looked down. A giant wave of water rolled over a lower deck.

Jack imagined water flooding the third-class corridor, the card room, and the grand staircase.

He closed his eyes, waiting to be washed away.

"*Arf! Arf!*"

The barking came from a distance.

"Teddy!" cried Annie.

Jack had forgotten all about the little dog.

Holding on to the railing, he used one hand to pull off his knapsack.

Teddy wasn't there!

There was more frantic barking.

"Where's Teddy?" cried Jack.

"He's calling us!" shouted Annie.

"We can't look for him!" shouted Jack. "We'll fall off the ship!"

Teddy barked and barked.

"He's close by!" said Annie.

She held on to the railing and moved slowly down the steep deck.

"Annie!" cried Jack.

Suddenly, the lights on the *Titanic* went out. The world was pitch-dark.

Jack couldn't see Annie at all.

"Annie!" he shouted.

He tried to move down the deck, too.

But the ship tilted again. Jack slipped and fell.

He rolled until he crashed into a smoke-stack.

"Jack!" cried Annie. "Here! Here!"

Teddy kept barking.

The back of the *Titanic* was rising out of the ocean. The front of the ship was going down.

Jack tried to go around the smokestack without falling.

In the dark, he could barely see the tree house. It was stuck between a smokestack and the railing. It was lying on its side.

Annie and Teddy were looking out the window.

"Teddy's barking led me here!" cried Annie. "Hurry, Jack!"

Jack crawled around the smokestack.

He held out his hand. Annie grabbed it. She pulled him into the tree house.

Teddy licked his face.

"I wish we could go home!" shouted Annie, pointing at the Pennsylvania book.

Jack heard a loud *CRA-A-A-ACK!*

The wind started to blow.

The tree house started to spin.

It spun faster and faster.

Then everything was still.

Absolutely still.

10

A Touch of Magic

"Oh, man," whispered Jack.

He was lying on the floor of the tree house. He was wearing his pajamas and rain poncho again.

"You okay?" Annie asked.

"Yeah. You?" said Jack.

"My heart's beating really fast," said Annie.

"Mine, too," said Jack.

He thought of the *Titanic* sinking into the

cold black sea. His eyes filled with tears.

"It was terrible," he said.

Annie nodded. Jack could see tears on her cheeks.

Teddy licked Jack's face.

"Hey," said Jack. "How did you get out of my knapsack?"

Teddy whined. Jack and Annie stroked his furry head and ears.

"I think he has a touch of magic," said Annie.

Slowly, Jack sat up.

"He saved our lives," he said.

"And now we have the first gift to break the spell he's under," said Annie.

She turned on her flashlight. She shined it on the silver pocket watch that hung from her neck.

"Lucy's gift," she said.

The watch had stopped. The hands were at 2:20.

Jack was silent. Then he sighed.

"That's exactly when the ship went down," he said.

Annie looked at him.

"I guess that's when time stopped for the *Titanic*," she said.

Jack nodded.

Annie put the pocket watch on top of Morgan's note.

"A gift from a ship lost at sea," she said softly.

They were both quiet.

Then Jack took off his glasses and wiped the tears from his eyes.

Annie stood up. She took a deep breath.

"I'm ready to go," she said. "Let's put Teddy in your pack and take him home with us."

She shined her flashlight around the tree house.

"Teddy?" she said.

There was no sign of the little dog.

"He's not here," said Annie.

"What are you talking about?" said Jack. "We were just petting him."

"He's up to his magic tricks again," said Annie. She sighed. "We'll have to go home without him."

"But what happened to him?" said Jack.

"I don't know," said Annie. "But I have a feeling we'll see him again soon."

She started down the rope ladder. Jack looked around the tree house one last time.

"Teddy?" he said.

But the tree house was quiet.

Jack pulled on his backpack and climbed down the rope ladder.

Annie was waiting for him.

Without a word, Jack took her hand.

The rain had stopped. But water still dripped from the trees.

Stars glittered overhead in a clear sky.

Silently, Jack and Annie left the Frog Creek woods. They walked up the dark street to their house and climbed the steps to their porch.

Before they went inside, they looked out again at the night.

"Time might have stopped for the *Titanic*," Jack said. "But books and memories keep the *Titanic* alive, don't they? It's a true story, but it's also like a myth now."

"Yeah," said Annie. "And every time the story's told, we wish it had a different ending."

Jack nodded. That was exactly how he felt.

Staring at the starry sky, he shuddered at the memory of the sinking ship.

He knew that he and Annie were lucky. They had come home.

"Good night, *Titanic*," he said softly. "Good-bye."

Then he and Annie slipped quietly into their house, where it was cozy and dry and very safe.

MORE FACTS FOR YOU AND JACK

1) The *Titanic* hit the iceberg in the North Atlantic, approximately 400 miles off the coast of Newfoundland.

2) The *Titanic* was considered unsinkable because she was built with huge watertight doors to contain any possible leaks. However, when the ship hit the iceberg, six watertight compartments quickly filled up with water, dooming the ship.

3) The signal SOS was chosen as an international distress call because of the simplicity of the three letters in Morse code: three dots, three dashes, and three dots.

4) No one knows for certain exactly how long the musicians played on the *Titanic*, but legend says they played until the ship went down, and their last song was the hymn "Nearer My God to Thee."

5) More than 1,500 people perished in the *Titanic* disaster, while 705 people escaped in lifeboats and were eventually rescued by a ship named the *Carpathia*.

6) After the sinking of the *Titanic*, laws were changed so that every ship was required to have enough lifeboats to carry *all* its passengers. Also, the International Ice Patrol was formed, so that ships would have warning about ice conditions.

7) In 1985, a scientist named Dr. Robert Ballard discovered the undersea wreck of the *Titanic*.

Don't miss the next Magic Tree House book,
when Jack and Annie go to the Great Plains
and find out how people in the Lakota tribe
lived.

MAGIC TREE HOUSE #18

BUFFALO
BEFORE BREAKFAST

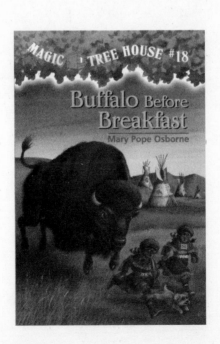

Where have you traveled in the

MAGIC TREE HOUSE ?

The Mystery of the Tree House
(Books #1–4)

❑ **Magic Tree House #1, DINOSAURS BEFORE DARK,** in which Jack and Annie discover the tree house and travel back to the time of dinosaurs.

❑ **Magic Tree House #2, THE KNIGHT AT DAWN,** in which Jack and Annie go to the time of knights and explore a medieval castle with a hidden passage.

❑ **Magic Tree House #3, MUMMIES IN THE MORNING,** in which Jack and Annie go to ancient Egypt and get lost in a pyramid when they help a ghost queen.

❑ **Magic Tree House #4, PIRATES PAST NOON,** in which Jack and Annie travel back in time and meet some unfriendly pirates searching for buried treasure.

The Mystery of the Magic Spell
(Books #5–8)

❑ **Magic Tree House #5, Night of the Ninjas,** in which Jack and Annie go to old Japan and learn the secrets of the ninjas.

❑ **Magic Tree House #6, Afternoon on the Amazon,** in which Jack and Annie explore the wild rain forest of the Amazon and are greeted by giant ants, hungry crocodiles, and flesh-eating piranhas.

❑ **Magic Tree House #7, Sunset of the Sabertooth,** in which Jack and Annie go back to the Ice Age—the world of woolly mammoths, sabertooth tigers, and a mysterious sorcerer.

❑ **Magic Tree House #8, Midnight on the Moon,** in which Jack and Annie go forward in time and explore the moon in a moon buggy.

The Mystery of the Ancient Riddles
(Books #9–12)

❑ **Magic Tree House #9, DOLPHINS AT DAYBREAK,** in which Jack and Annie arrive on a coral reef, where they find a mini-submarine that takes them underwater into the world of sharks and dolphins.

❑ **Magic Tree House #10, GHOST TOWN AT SUNDOWN,** in which Jack and Annie travel to the Wild West, where they battle horse thieves, meet a kindly cowboy, and get some help from a mysterious ghost.

❑ **Magic Tree House #11, LIONS AT LUNCHTIME,** in which Jack and Annie go to the plains of Africa, where they help wild animals cross a rushing river and have a picnic with a Masai warrior.

❑ **Magic Tree House #12, POLAR BEARS PAST BEDTIME,** in which Jack and Annie go to the Arctic, where they get help from a seal hunter, play with polar bear cubs, and get trapped on thin ice.

The Mystery of the Lost Stories
(Books #13–16)

❑ **Magic Tree House #13, VACATION ON THE VOLCANO,** in which Jack and Annie land in Pompeii during Roman times, on the very day Mount Vesuvius erupts!

❑ **Magic Tree House #14, DAY OF THE DRAGON KING,** in which Jack and Annie travel back to ancient China, where they must face an emperor who burns books.

❑ **Magic Tree House #15, VIKING SHIPS AT SUNRISE,** in which Jack and Annie visit a monastery in medieval Ireland on the day the Vikings attack!

❑ **Magic Tree House #16, HOUR OF THE OLYMPICS,** in which Jack and Annie are whisked back to ancient Greece and the first Olympic games.